JOHNNY APPLESEED

THE GRAND OLD MAN OF THE FOREST

Retold by
MARGARET HENLEY

Illustrated by
RICHARD MADISON

Cavendish Square
New York

A long time ago, when America was still a very young country, there was a man who everyone knew as Johnny Appleseed. His hair was long and black, and his eyes were blue and full of energy. His real name was John Chapman, but people don't call him that anymore.

When John was barely two years old, his mother died, and his father married another woman. John began to live with his grandmother, who had many apple trees in her garden. Little John loved to watch the pretty flowers on the trees slowly change into delicious fruit.

When John was eighteen, he left his grandmother's home. He wanted to travel and see the world. This is when his adventures began!

Many people were traveling from the East toward the West at that time in search of more land. John decided to go with them. He loved traveling, discovering new places, meeting new people, and exploring new areas.

But most of the travelers would soon find a clear spot and settle down! John was very upset. “Oh, no!” he thought. “I would never be able to live my whole life in one place! What should I do now?”

John noticed that many people settling down were having a hard time farming land that had never been cultivated before. John had an idea. “Hey! What if I plant trees before the settlers get here?” he thought. “That way, they don’t need to bother cultivating the land, and I don’t have to settle down!”

Now John was faced with a question. Which type of tree should he plant? There were so many to choose from! Can you guess which tree he chose to plant in these lands? That's right! He thought of all the delicious things that could be made out of apples and decided to plant apple trees wherever he could.

And so, John would move West ahead of the travelers and find nice, fertile land. He would clear it and sow the seeds himself. He would then build a fence around the trees to protect them from wild animals. And as the trees grew, John would sell them to the settlers when they arrived. If any tree remained unsold, he would come back periodically to tend to it.

When the settlers came, they were welcomed by the familiar apple trees. They could eat pies, make apple butter, and even drink cider! Before then, they were forced to eat fish and meat every day. Can you imagine eating the same thing day in and day out?

John would often walk down the road with a huge sack of seeds swung over his back, sowing apple trees along the way. One day a little boy saw him and shouted, “Ma! Look! Johnny Appleseed is here. He’s planting more trees.” The name stuck, and after that everyone called him Johnny Appleseed.

Johnny had a dream. He wished that no one in America would ever go hungry. He wanted to plant enough apple trees to feed everyone. Many poor people could not afford food. He would give them his apples and apple seeds for free.

Johnny didn't have a home of his own. "The Earth is my home, and the sky is my roof," he would say. He loved sleeping in the forest under the starry sky. If the weather was bad, he would ask for shelter from a family in exchange for apple seeds. Even then, he would sleep on the floor near the fireplace. Everyone welcomed him with open arms.

On most days, he stayed out in the wild, without carrying a gun or knife. "Animals are creatures of God. They will not harm me," he would say.

Johnny would eat his meals outdoors. He was a vegetarian, and usually ate only fruit and nuts.

Not many things could make Johnny angry, but wasting food was one thing he couldn't bear. He said, "If no one were to waste any food, there would be enough for everyone to eat."

Johnny was also very kind to all animals. Some people said that he could even understand their language! In fact, before lighting a fire, he would check logs for worms, ants, and other insects so that he could shake them off before he burned the wood. In spite of living in the wild for most of his life, not once did he kill an animal.

One day, Johnny went to visit his friend, Whitney. Whitney greeted him with a gun in his hand. He was all set for a hunting expedition. “Johnny! What a pleasant surprise! I was just on my way to go hunting. Why don’t you join me? It will be fun!” he said.

Johnny was very upset. He did not believe that man had the right to end another creature’s life. After a long argument, Whitney was forced to agree and put his gun away.

People would often say that Johnny Appleseed was quite eccentric because one could see him walking around barefoot, wearing nothing but a large sack as clothes, with holes for his arms and head. Instead of a hat, he wore a tin pot on his head, which he also used for cooking.

One day, a farmer's wife gave him some clothes and shoes. Johnny was about to wear them when he saw a poor old man shivering on the road. "Poor man!" he thought to himself. "He has nowhere to go. He will surely die if I leave him here like this." So Johnny gave his new clothes away to the old man.

Johnny loved playing with children. He saw that many children did not know how to read. So in every settlement he visited, he carried with him a book. He would tear the pages and distribute among children, teaching them how to read.

Johnny was very friendly with the Native Americans. They liked him for his kind ways and love of nature.

Johnny gave them some of his saplings, and they taught him the healing powers of herbs and other plants. During his travels among the settlers, if he ever came across a sick child or someone in need, he would heal them.

In those days, the settlers and Native Americans were at war with each other. Johnny Appleseed, though, was friendly with both sides. Once, when he heard that the Native Americans were planning to attack the settlers, he ran bareheaded and barefoot all night for thirty miles to get the settlers help.

Johnny bought things only if he needed them. Once, he bought a herd of ponies to help him carry his load of apple seeds. Suddenly, a tribe of Native Americans captured him and stole his ponies. "It's okay," he thought to himself. "Things happen for a reason. I'm sure they needed the ponies more than I did."

Once, Johnny was sitting in the fields and eating, when a snake tried to bite him on the foot. Legend says that his skin had become so tough from the cold and wind that the fangs of the snake could not pierce his skin! In fact, living outdoors had made his skin so tough that he was known to amuse children by pressing hot coals or needles to the soles of his feet, without feeling a thing!

People say that he once survived a cold, snowy night by digging a hole in the snow and using it as shelter.

One day, when Johnny was seventy years old, he knocked on the door of an old friend, William Worth. “Old friend, I don’t feel too well,” he said. “May I please take shelter here for the night?”

“Of course you may,” said William. “What can I get you to eat?”

“Just some milk and bread will be fine,” said Johnny.

After his evening meal, as per his custom, he read aloud from the Bible, curled up on the floor near the fireplace, and never woke up.

The quirky old man with the tin pot on his head was never seen walking down the road again. He was missed by all. Children missed playing with him, and farmers missed his help.

For fifty years of his life, Johnny roamed the wilderness planting trees. If we were to count all the trees he planted, they would cover more than a hundred thousand square miles. Many of these trees remain there even today.

So the next time you are eating an apple, think of Johnny Appleseed. It might just have come from one of the trees that old Johnny planted!

ABOUT JOHNNY APPLESEED

Though it is easy to confuse the story of Johnny Appleseed with a folktale, John Chapman is, in fact, a historic figure. He was born in Leominster, Massachusetts in 1774. His father served in the American Revolution, and John was the second of three children. He had two siblings and ten half-siblings, making the grand total twelve!

Over time, fact and fiction have become intertwined. Though history has a record of John Chapman, the smart, yet benevolent nomadic businessman, it is fun to remember him as Johnny Appleseed, the quirky old animal whisperer who wore a sack to cover his body, and a tin pot to cover his head.

WORDS TO KNOW

Cultivate: To prepare land for growing crops.

Eccentric: A person with an odd, or unusual, personality.

Saplings: Before plants grow into trees, they are called saplings. They are in fact baby plants.

Settlers: When European pioneers first landed in America, they all settled down along the East Coast. Over time, they slowly began moving West and settling down. These people were known as settlers.

Vegetarian: Someone who eats only plants, not meat. Though this is a common occurrence now, it was almost unheard of in those days for someone to choose not to eat meat.

TO FIND OUT MORE

BOOKS:

Kellogg, Steven. *Johnny Appleseed.* New York: Morrow Junior Books, 1988.

Yolen, Jane; Burke, Jim. *Johnny Appleseed: The Legend and Truth.* New York: HarperCollins, 2008.

WEBSITES:

http://americanfolklore.net/folklore/2010/08/johnny_appleseed.html

Storyteller S.E. Schlosser retells this fascinating legend from Ohio.

http://www.bestapples.com/kids/teachers/johnny.shtml

This site tries to separate fact from fiction. There is also a fun crossword that you can solve at the end!

http://esl-bits.net/listening/Media/2012-08-19/Johnny_Appleseed/

You can listen to and read about how Johnny Appleseed became a folk hero on this site.

Published in 2014 by Cavendish Square Publishing, LLC
303 Park Avenue South, Suite 1247, New York, NY 10010

First Edition

CPSIA Compliance Information: Batch #WW14CSQ
All websites were available and accurate when this book was sent to press.
LIBRARY OF CONGRESS CATALOGING-IN-PUBLICATION DATA
Benjamin, Margaret.
Johnny Appleseed/Margaret Benjamin.
pages cm. — (American legends and folktales)
ISBN 978-1-62712-277-1 (hardcover) ISBN 978-1-62712-278-8 (paperback) ISBN 978-1-62712-279-5 (ebook)
1. Appleseed, Johnny, 1774-1845—Juvenile literature. 2. Apple growers—United States—Biography—Juvenile literature. 3. Frontier and pioneer life—Middle West—Juvenile literature.
I. Title.
SB63.C46B47 2014
634.11092—dc23

Printed in the United States of America

Editorial Director: Dean Miller
Art Director: Jeffrey Talbot

Content and Design by quadrum®
www.quadrumltd.com